PUFFIN CANADA

THE GRYPHON PROJECT

CARRIE MAC is an award-winning author who lives in Pemberton, British Columbia. Her first novel, *The Beckoners*, won the Arthur Ellis YA Award and the Stellar Award, and is a CLA Honour book. *The Droughtlanders*, the first book in the Triskelia series, was shortlisted for the Sunburst Award and the White Pine, and was a nominee for the Young Adult Library Services Association–Best Book. It was also shortlisted for the CLA Young Adult Award, along with *Retribution* and *Storm*.

PUFFIN CANADA

Published by the Penguin Group

Penguin Group (Canada), 90 Eglinton Avenue East, Suite 700, Toronto, Ontario, Canada M4P 2Y3
(a division of Pearson Canada Inc.)

Penguin Group (USA) Inc., 375 Hudson Street, New York, New York 10014, U.S.A.
Penguin Books Ltd, 80 Strand, London WC2R 0RL, England
Penguin Ireland, 25 St Stephen's Green, Dublin 2, Ireland (a division of Penguin Books Ltd)
Penguin Group (Australia), 250 Camberwell Road, Camberwell, Victoria 3124, Australia
(a division of Pearson Australia Group Pty Ltd)
Penguin Books India Pvt Ltd, 11 Community Centre, Panchsheel Park, New Delhi – 110 017, India
Penguin Group (NZ), 67 Apollo Drive, Rosedale, North Shore 0745, Auckland, New Zealand
(a division of Pearson New Zealand Ltd)
Penguin Books (South Africa) (Pty) Ltd, 24 Sturdee Avenue, Rosebank,
Johannesburg 2196, South Africa

Penguin Books Ltd, Registered Offices: 80 Strand, London WC2R 0RL, England

First published 2009

1 2 3 4 5 6 7 8 9 10 (WEB)

Copyright © Carrie Mac, 2009

Manufactured in Canada.

LIBRARY AND ARCHIVES CANADA CATALOGUING IN PUBLICATION

Mac, Carrie, 1975-
The Gryphon project / Carrie Mac.

ISBN 978-0-14-316814-0

I. Title.
PS8625.A23G79 2009   jC813'.6   C2009-901362-2

Visit the Penguin Group (Canada) website at **www.penguin.ca**

Special and corporate bulk purchase rates available; please see
www.penguin.ca/corporatesales or call 1-800-810-3104, ext. 477 or 474

FOR CARLA POPPEN ...
WISE WOMAN, CHERISHED CRONE.

THE OLD GRYPH

For the longest time, Phoenix's older brother, Gryphon, had been her favourite person in the whole world. In Grade 4 she'd had to write an essay about her number-one hero, and she'd chosen Gryph. She'd written five pages about how great he was, even though the assignment was for only two hundred words. And she'd illustrated it too, drawing Gryph as a superhero flying through the air with a crimson cape, and herself standing on the grass far below, waving up at him.

He was the perfect big brother. Older by two and a half years, he always hung out with her when he had a chance, never complaining when she wanted to play tea party or house or dress-up. He didn't mind her tagging along when he hung out with his friends, cheering her on when they played soccer, or lifting her up on the basketball court so she could get a slam dunk. He latched on to a trio of best friends in kindergarten, and so over the years Saul and Huy and Tariq became like brothers to her too. And she and Nadia—her own best friend since preschool—were like sisters to them all. The boys watched out for them, and as the girls finally made it to high school and Saul started dating Nadia, the whole gang of them were still super close. Even Neko, Nadia's little brother, had been welcomed into Gryph's enchanted circle. He was almost four years younger than the boys, and two years younger than the girls. He was their mascot.

AND THROUGH IT ALL, Gryph was climbing up the ladder of fame. He was a gifted athlete, and a favourite of the media. Even when he was still playing T-ball and peewee hockey, his was the picture that made it into the back pages of the sports section. And slowly, his picture started making it to the front page of the sports section. But still, he was always happy to be with the family. He was that cool older brother, the smart and athletic son who genuinely liked his parents and his little sisters too. He was the guy who would make the popcorn on a Friday night and divvy it into bowls as the others got settled for yet another cheesy movie suitable for six-year-old Fawn. He was the guy who would watch *Chitty Chitty Bang Bang* over and over and still not grumble about it. He was the guy who would piggyback his littlest sister up to bed and then play three games of chess with Phee at the coffee table while their father read his pile of novels and Eva went over her files from work. He was the guy Phee looked up to. Or he had been. Until about a year ago.

SHE WATCHED HIM NOW, trying to place when she'd first noticed the change. He shoved his baseball gear into an enormous duffle bag, his face frozen in his usual look as of late. Anger. Or just plain darkness, Phee couldn't tell what it was exactly. He glanced up and saw her sitting at the top of the stairs.

"What?" He scowled at her.

"Where're you going?"

"Saul's."

"You have practice on a Friday night? What about our movie night?" Actually, Phee couldn't remember the last time Gryph had been home on a Friday night. "Fawn misses you." What she meant was that *she* missed him. But she wouldn't say that to his face, not with him glaring at her like that.

"We have practice in the morning." Gryph shoved his cleats into the bag and fought with the zipper. "Not that it's any of your business."

"Can Nadia and I come watch?"

"Why?"

"She likes to swoon over Saul, and I've got nothing better to do." Gryph shrugged. "What do I care?"

"Got that right," Phee mumbled.

"What did you say?"

"Nothing."

"Sure sounded like a bitchy sort of nothing." Gryph hefted the bag onto his shoulder and made his way down the front walk.

PHOENIX SET HER CHIN on her fist and watched him cross the green, making his way to the train station. Who was that guy? He looked like Gryph, and lived Gryph's life, but he wasn't the Gryph she knew. The Gryph she knew would've gladly invited her to come watch. He used to be her friend. But now he was just an asshole who lived in her house. And hardly that, he spent the night at Saul's as often as he could. Even school nights. Her parents wouldn't let Phee stay over at Nadia's on a school night, but somehow Gryph had convinced them that because Saul's house was closer to school and Gryph's various sports practices, it was okay. When Phee claimed that was unfair, her mother told her she knew full well that girls stayed up all night chatting, while boys actually slept. Phee wasn't so sure about that.

And besides, it was categorically unfair. Phee was still bitter about it. When she'd accused her parents of using a double standard, they had asked her if she would actually *sleep* at Nadia's, and she had to say no. She was not one to lie to Oscar and Eva. She genuinely loved and trusted them, even if Gryph didn't lately.

THE WEIRD THING was that he was still super sweet to Fawn. Almost as if he were trying to hide his new mean self from her. Maybe Fawn was his new favourite sister.

Phee wished things could go back to the way they were before.

Maybe it was the stress of being a champion athlete. Gryph was sponsored by Chrysalis, which came with a lot of pressure, sure, but a lot of perks too. The media attention, the high-tech gear, the fame.

The fame.

Maybe that was it? Ever since he'd won the X Games last year he'd changed. Maybe all the hype had turned him into a prick.

Phee never knew if it was going to be a Good Gryph day or a Bad Gryph day, and so it had her walking on eggshells. She missed the old Gryphon. She missed his easy laugh and his carefree approach to anything life threw at him.

And he wasn't training as hard anymore, even though he was still winning. He just didn't seem to care about it as much. He'd signed a ten-year contract with Chrysalis almost three years ago. It was meant to see him through college and into the pros, for whichever sport he ended up choosing. He was good at them all. There were a lot of years left on that contract. Phee wasn't sure if she could stand seven more years of this Gryphon.

PHEE WATCHED HER BROTHER until he was out of sight, and then she went inside to find her father. He was in his study, writing his sermon for Sunday. Phee plopped down in one of the easy chairs he kept across from the desk for when he counselled parishioners. His United Church served three suburbs and was located in the farthest one out, so sometimes it was easier for people to meet him at home rather than go all the way to the church.

"Do you think Gryph is on drugs?" She didn't really believe this, because how could he still pass all those substance tests? On the other hand, he was smart. Maybe there was a way?

"Gryph? Drugs?" Oscar looked up, surprised. "Where did that come from?"

"He's just been so weird lately."

"He's a teenager—"

"So am I!"

"He's not you." Oscar shrugged. He set aside his highlighted Bible, holding his place with a paper clip. "He's a boy."

"That's an excuse?"

"He's older?" Oscar grinned. "Is that a better excuse? He's charting the waters for you and Fawn?"

"I won't ever be like that."

"Like what?" He was using his minister voice on her, calm and inquisitive.

"Rude. Aloof." Phee tried to think of a better way to explain it, but it was more an unsettling feeling than anything she could pinpoint.

The worst part, though, was that Gryph was keeping secrets. How did she know this? Because he often had a look about him, as if he'd just done something bad. The same look their dog, Riley, had after he'd stolen something off the counter—back when he was nimble enough to reach, that is.

And Phee had a sick sense that it would be the secrets that would get him in trouble. Trouble he might not ever come out of. Life-and-death-sized trouble.

"The answer is no."

"Huh?" Phee broke from her thoughts.

"Huh?"

"Sorry, excuse me?"

"No, I don't think he's on drugs." Oscar made a note on his pad before looking up at her again. "And even if he wasn't tested regularly, I'd still say no."

"Why?"

"Because your mother and I trust your brother to make smart choices, just the way we trust you to do the same."

Phee said nothing more after that. She curled up in the chair and stared at the ceiling tiles for a long moment, all the while wondering why she didn't trust Gryph anymore if her parents still did.

"How're you doing, kiddo?"

"Me?"

"No, not you. The four-headed, goggle-eyed monster sitting in the corner with his finger up his nose." Oscar laughed. "Of course you. Considering tomorrow's anniversary."

Tomorrow. Right. Fifteen years ago tomorrow, Phoenix had died. For the first time. And fifteen years ago tomorrow, the Chrysalis Corporation had brought her back from the dead.

DEATHDAY

Phee went to sleep with her first death on her mind but had banished the subject by morning. Usually she was pretty good at that, putting it out of her mind. If she didn't, she could lose entire days to dwelling on it. She got up, had breakfast, and went to meet Nadia at her house. Nadia insisted on going to watch the boys' baseball practice, never mind that Phee had told her Gryph didn't particularly want them there.

"So?" Nadia asked as she finished up her makeup on the train. "Gryph's not the boss of me. I'm going to watch Saul in his tight little uniform, not Mister Stick-Up-His-Ass Gryphon Nicholson-Lalonde."

Phee laughed, happy to launch into another what's-wrong-with-Gryph session, but Nadia nipped that in the bud by handing her an envelope. With a sinking feeling, Phee realized what it was. Nadia was the only person who ever acknowledged the day she died. Because she had two such days, Phee could expect a little something from Nadia to stir up bad feelings twice a year.

"Happy deathday," Nadia said. "You thought I'd forgotten, didn't you?"

"You never forget." Phee wished she had the heart to tell Nadia how her cards and gifts turned her stomach into knots and made her fixate on what had happened. But Nadia had only good intentions, and Phee would hate to hurt her feelings, so she never said anything about it.

Phee slid a finger under the envelope's flap. Inside was a homemade card with a cartoon baby in a coffin on the front, with X's for eyes and a thin grey line for a mouth. She opened the card. The same baby was now sitting in a field of flowers with a grin on her face and rosy circles on her cheeks. On the opposite side Nadia had spelled her name in glue and then doused the card with pink glitter so the glitter would stick in the shape of her name. *Phoenix!* it bellowed cheerfully. Below it, Nadia had written in her elaborate cursive, *"My bestest friend Phee ... what would I do without you? I'm so glad that you're still here. Much love on your deathday, xoxo, Nadia ... your bestest friend for almost twelve years, even if you don't remember it all."*

"I realize it looks kind of weird, like I meant it to be funny or something." Nadia leaned over and blew some extra glitter onto the floor of the train. "But I'm serious. I'm so glad you're still alive." She hugged Phee. "I really don't know what I'd do without you."

Phee stared at the card.

"You like it?"

"Of course." Phee forced a grin. "It is kind of creepy, with the X's for eyes. But I like it."

"Good!"

"Thanks, Nadia. It's very thoughtful."

"Oh, and I got you this." Nadia rummaged in her purse and pulled out a short slender box. Her expensive brand of mascara. "It's in the perfect colour for you. Like a really dark eggplant purple. It'll look amazing with your green eyes. Swear it."

With that, she pulled her own mascara from her purse and went to work finishing her eyes while Phee was once again trapped in the awful spinny feeling that came with every deathday reminder. A constant dark, humming circle of *what if, what if, what if?*

THE FIRST TIME Phoenix died, she'd only been six months old, just. She'd been born too early, her lungs underdeveloped and prone to infections. The Chrysalis Corporation was the one and only organization authorized to perform recons, and they did not recon babies under six months. This was written into law via their Spiritual Agreement, drawn up with the Multi-faith Congress, which Phoenix's father had been a board member of long before Phee's traumatic birth. In her first few precarious months, he'd pleaded his family's case and proposed addenda to the law, but even he had to admit that the age restriction served a purpose. There had to be limits. And after all, he'd helped write the law in the first place.

But his wife hated every word of that law. Every night she would badger him about the Congress, beg him to make them understand, just this once. Just for their daughter. Phoenix knew that her difficult first six months almost ended her parents' marriage, as they battled over the ethics of reconning babies younger than the law allowed. Oscar's mantra was "If she dies, of course we'll mourn ... of *course*, Eva. But it's God's will." Her mother—a physician—always retorted, "And your very same God gave us the brains and science to challenge his will"—big dramatic Eva-like pause—"and so we should."

Of course, ethics aside, both Oscar and Eva fought for their little girl to live. Eva took a leave from her practice and cared for Phoenix at home. She and Oscar hired a private respiratory therapist to be at her bedside twenty-four hours a day. On the day Phoenix turned exactly six months old, the respiratory therapist was let go, the machines were turned off, and her mother and father held her in their arms while she struggled for breath. Her mother sang lullabies, and her father prayed, until she was too tired to breathe anymore and she died.

And what about Gryphon? Her beloved older brother would've been turning three, just a toddler himself. Phee thought he should've been there as the respirator and tubes were removed, as Oscar lifted her from her little cot. She thought he should've been with her parents as they cried and held her as she died. She had a memory of Gryphon holding her tiny hand as it paled to blue. But it was a false memory. She had no memory from that time. It was just something that her heart made up because it felt good. Much better than knowing that he wasn't there at all. He was eating macaroni and cheese at their grandparents' house, his swim shorts still wet from running through the sprinkler, his mouth topped with a chocolate milk moustache.

He hadn't seen Phoenix die. He hadn't experienced his own grief or confusion, or witnessed his parents' sadness as the colour drained from her baby cheeks. He didn't see their tears as her chest rose and fell, slower, slower, until she was still. He hadn't heard their parents crying as they waited for Chrysalis's shuttle that would come to collect her body.

Maybe things would've turned out differently if he'd been there.

PHEE DIDN'T REMEMBER watching the baseball practice, or the fact that it had started to rain. When she finally broke from going over what she knew of her first death, she was walking across the field with Nadia and the boys, in the direction of the restaurant where they often ate after. She pulled up the hood of her jacket and wiped her cheeks, wet from the summer drizzle. Tariq glanced back at her as she did. He gave her a look that silently asked if she was all right, so she gave him a little nod back. He never said much, but he didn't have to. Phee wished that Gryph still cared, or acted as if he did.

She cornered her brother as he held the restaurant door open for the others. Phee hung back until it was just the two of them.

"You know what day it is?"

"Saturday."

"But what's special about it?"

Gryph shrugged. "Enlighten me. You clearly want to."

"It's my deathday."

"Right." Gryph rolled his eyes. "You know Mom and Dad think it isn't healthy when you dwell on it. Guess what?"

Phee waited for the inevitable.

"You're dwelling." He turned to go into the restaurant, but Phee grabbed his arm.

"Wait. Gryph, please."

He let the door close, and it was once again just the two of them in the rain. "Go."

"Did Mom and Dad talk about me? When I was dead?"

"Of course they did. Your recon was pretty much all they talked about." Gryph glanced inside, where the others had set up at a table near the window. "Okay?"

"Did you miss me?"

"I guess. Although you weren't much fun to begin with, being so sick. And just a baby."

"Did you understand, though? Did you get what was happening?"

"Sure I understood."

But how could he have understood? Phee tried to imagine their little sister at three, remembering. It didn't seem likely. "You were only little."

"I remember what it's like to be three," Gryph snapped. "You don't. So I'll decide what I do and don't remember, if you don't mind." He flung open the door to let a family trickle out, the two little kids squealing at the rain, the parents arguing about the bill. Phee watched them dash across to the train station, all of them in short sleeves, running from the rain. When she turned back, Gryph had gone inside. She watched through the window as he slid into the booth, all grin and charm for his friends. And there was Phee, outside as usual, in more ways than one.

IF IT HADN'T BEEN for Nadia's stupid card, Phee could've slid through the day in blessed denial. But her first death still weighed heavily on her that night. She wandered around the house—the same house in which she'd died that first time—finally stopping in the door of the laundry room, where her mother was folding a load out of the dryer.

"Know what day it is?" Phee leaned her head against the doorframe, the weight of the day giving her a headache.

Eva folded one of Fawn's pink shirts and set it on a pile. "Of course." She went to the door and pulled Phee into a tight hug. "Of course I do."

"Do you think Gryph remembers when it happened?"

"Sure." Her mother nodded as she went back to the laundry. "He's always had a brilliant memory."

That stung. But Phee knew her mother didn't mean it to.

"I used to find him in your room, looking in the crib. 'Where my sister?' he'd ask, 'Where my Phee go?'"

"What did you tell him?"

Eva picked up one of Fawn's little sweatshirts and hugged it absent-mindedly to her chest. "I told him that you'd died. I told him you'd be back when the scientists were finished reconning you."

"Did he understand what that meant?"

"Well, not really. I explained that reconning was something that scientists did to bring people back from the dead, when they decide that it's not their time to go. But then your father complicated matters by bringing God into it. He told Gryph that God was the one who decided when it was people's time to die or come back."

Phee had heard this all before, but she listened as if for the first time. Each word her mother spoke of that time brought Phee closer to the little girl she'd been and lost. Twice.

"Even though we'd agreed on how to explain it to Gryphon." Eva smiled. "But you know how your father is. We got into quite the discussion, as I recall. We were walking Gryphon to the park, maybe a day or two after you'd died. I was so mad that his all-powerful God hadn't made you stronger to begin with. And he was frustrated that I couldn't allow God to be fallible." Eva gave a small, sad laugh and hugged the sweatshirt even tighter to her. "And then the next thing we knew Gryph had bolted ahead of us and had climbed to the top of the swing set. Your dad grabbed his ankle just before he would've fallen. It wasn't a good day." Eva closed her eyes, remembering. "Not a good day at all."

"Mom," Gryph said from right behind Phee. "You always forget to mention Riley in that story."

Phee spun around. How long had he been standing there? Gryph grinned at her. "What?"

"You're eavesdropping!"

"It's my house too."

"Only when you feel like it."

"Whatever." Gryph shrugged. "But Riley was there too. He barked, remember?"

"He did," Eva said. "You're right."

"He barked, and that's what made you look up from your fight—"

"Discussion, Gryph."

"*Fight*, Mother." Gryph cocked his head at Eva. "He was just a puppy, but he was smart. He knew I was going to fall."

Hearing his name, the big old mutt pushed himself off his comfy bed by the kitchen door and hobbled over to the laundry room, his tail wagging. Riley leaned against Phee's leg and gazed up at her, as if silently recounting his own version of events from that day so long ago.